The Brave Servant

A TALE FROM CHINA

Retold by Suzanne I. Barchers
Illustrated by Yu-mei Han

RED CHAIR PRESS

Please visit our website at **www.redchairpress.com**.
Find a free catalog of all our high-quality products for young readers.

 For a free activity page for this story, go to
www.redchairpress.com and look for Free Activities.

The Brave Servant

Publisher's Cataloging-In-Publication Data
(Prepared by The Donohue Group, Inc.)

Barchers, Suzanne I.
The brave servant : a tale from China / retold by Suzanne I. Barchers ;
illustrated by Yu-mei Han.
p. : col. ill. ; cm. -- (Tales of honor)
Summary: The Lord of Luchow is a kind man. However, when he and his people
are threatened with war, a brave and loyal servant finds a way to protect his master
and bring peace to the lands. Includes special educational sections: Words to know,
What do you think?, and About China.
Interest age level: 006-010.
ISBN: 978-1-937529-73-4 (lib. binding/hardcover)
ISBN: 978-1-937529-57-4 (pbk.)
ISBN: 978-1-936163-89-2 (eBook)
1. Courage--Juvenile fiction. 2. Loyalty--Juvenile fiction. 3. Indentured servants--
Juvenile fiction. 4. War--Juvenile fiction. 5. Folklore--China. 6. Courage--Fiction.
7. Loyalty--Fiction. 8. Indentured servants--Fiction. 9. War--Fiction.
10. Folklore--China. I. Han, Yu-Mei. II. Title.

PZ8.1.B37 Br 2013

398.2/73/0951   2012951559

This series first published by:
Red Chair Press LLC   PO Box 333   South Egremont, MA 01258-0333

Printed in the United States of America

1 2 3 4 5 18 17 16 15 14

Long ago, one man governed many districts
in Luchow in China. The Lord of Luchow had a
large household with many servants to care for
it. One servant, Jun, had learned to read. He also
played the lute and was skilled in the art of magic.
This was most unusual for servants of the time.

One night the lord held a grand feast. During the feast, Jun heard the steady beating of a kettledrum. He listened carefully to the tense drumbeats. Then he spoke to his lord.

"My lord," he said, bowing low. "Please accept my apologies for interrupting your feast. But I have been listening to the drumbeats. They have an edge of sadness to them. There seems to be something troubling the drummer. Would you be kind enough to speak with him?"

The lord, a gentle man, sent for the drummer. "Is something wrong? Your drumming sounds sad."

"Ah," the drummer replied. "You are right, my lord. My wife just died, and I would like to take her body to her homeland for burial. But I am in your service and feared asking for leave."

"Young man, I am sorry for your loss," the lord said. "You have my permission to take your wife to her final resting place."

The drummer left, praising the lord for his kindness. The lord realized he had an unusual servant.

The days passed pleasantly. Jun worked hard serving his master. He was organizing papers in the reception room when a messenger arrived. Jun listened to the report given to the lord.

"My lord, I have grave news for you," the messenger said.

"Speak freely. What is the trouble?" the Lord of Luchow asked.

The messenger spoke quietly. "The Lord of Weipu has gathered a large army. They are strong and well-trained. They are especially good at martial arts."

"This is indeed distressing," the Lord of Luchow replied. "War would be devastating to our people. Thank you for bringing this to me. I know it was not easy to bring such troubling news."

The Lord of Luchow was a peace-loving man.
Still, he gathered his army and set up tents
outside the city. By night he lay awake in his
tent and worried. By day he could not even eat.
All he could do was worry about safeguarding
his people.

Among Jun's few possessions was a jeweled sword with beautiful engravings. Jun decided it was time to put his skills in the art of magic to work. He slipped into his room and put on dark clothes.

He retrieved the sword from its case
and murmured a few words over it.
And then the wind lifted him up and
carried him away.

Jun flew through the black night until he could see the dying embers of the enemy campfire. He hovered over the sentries, noting that they drowsed in the heavy night air. He let the wind lower him to the ground. Then he sneaked past the sentries, searching for the tent of the Lord of Weipu.

Finding a large tent, Jun slipped inside. He looked around while the lord snored gently. Soon Jun spied a golden urn sitting near the bed. He tucked it under his arm and left.

Once past the sentries, he murmured his magic words over the sword. Once again, he drifted on the wind all the way back to Luchow.

Jun went directly to his master's tent where the lord was wide awake, worrying as usual.

"My lord, forgive this intrusion," Jun said. "I have just been to the enemy's camp. I have taken this golden urn."

"Jun! That was a brave, but foolish, thing to do. Once the theft has been discovered, they will surely attack."

"I have a plan," Jun said. "Send a messenger
with the urn to their camp in the morning.
He should tell the Lord of Weipu that you are
returning it with your compliments. Trust me."

The Lord of Luchow was baffled. Yet he trusted
his servant and sent for the messenger.

Early the next morning, a messenger arrived at the tent of the Lord of Weipu. The messenger bowed low and set the urn at his feet. "Lord, I have come from the camp of the Lord of Luchow. He sends this urn with his compliments."

The lord's mind raced as he stared at the urn. He had his guard escort the messenger out of the camp. Then he sent for his general.

"Something disturbing has just occurred," he said quietly. "This urn was removed from my tent as I slept last night. Now, it would have been easy to take my life along with this urn. Instead, the Lord of Luchow returned the urn along with his greetings."

"Lord," his general said, "they must have great power if they can do this."

"I agree," the Lord of Weipu replied. "I see only one thing to do."

The next day, the Lord of Luchow received a message. He read it carefully and then sent for Jun.

"Good morning, my lord," said Jun. "How may I be of service to you?"

"Jun, it seems you have done all of our people a fine service already. I have just received this message from the Lord of Weipu. Would you like to read it?"

Jun took the letter and read it aloud. "To the Lord of Luchow. With grace and honor you have spared my life and returned my urn. I pledge to you that I will devote the rest of my life to you. Your faithful servant, The Lord of Weipu."

And from that day forward, Jun and the people of Luchow enjoyed peace and prosperity.

WORDS TO KNOW

compliments: polite expressions of praise or friendship

hovered: remain suspended in the air over something

marital arts: various skills of self-defense such as judo, karate, or kendo

sentries: soldiers stationed to guard or control access to a place

WHAT DO YOU THINK?

Question 1: Why do you think the Lord of Luchow trusted his servant Jun?

Question 2: How do you know the Lord of Luchow was a kind leader? Can you think of more than one example from the story?

Question 3: Why did Jun steal the golden urn from the Lord of Weipu's tent?

Question 4: The Lord of Weipu did not engage in war with the Lord of Luchow. Do you think he was afraid he would lose? Why else might the Lord of Weipu have backed down from a battle?

About China

With one of the oldest recorded histories, China is rich in stories of the past. *The Brave Servant* is a tale that may have originated during the Ming Dynasty (14th-17th Centuries). During this dynasty, the rulers built a system of urban centers and rural farms. For most of the 270 years, it was a prosperous time. This tale is thought to have been told as a way to remind people that the old system of regional lords was filled jealousy and fighting.

About the Author

After fifteen years as a teacher, Suzanne Barchers began a career in writing and publishing. She has written over 100 children's books, two college textbooks, and more than 20 reader's theater and teacher resource books. She previously held editorial roles at Weekly Reader and LeapFrog and is on the PBS Kids Media Advisory Board. Suzanne also plays the flute professionally – and for fun – from her home in Stanford, CA.

About the Illustrator

Yu-mei Han wanted to be an artist as a young girl. She earned her fine arts degree from a university in Taiwan. Now Yu-mei illustrates books and magazines as well as greeting cards and wrapping paper. She currently lives in Queens, New York, with her husband and her dog Mollie.